Pirates and Dinosaurs

Irene Farримond

Pirates and Dinosaurs

IRENE FARRIMOND

© Irene Farrimond 2010

Published by Three White Foxes

ISBN 978-0-9565739-0-2

Prepared and printed by
York Publishing Services Ltd
64 Hallfield Road
Layerthorpe
York
YO31 7ZQ
www.yps-publishing.co.uk

CONTENTS

CHAPTER 1

Whitby

"Are we there yet?" asked Olivia as she rubbed her eyes. She had slept for most of the journey and was now looking out of the car window in the hope of seeing the sea.

"It's not far now," replied Mum, "look for the Abbey, the first one to see it gets a pound!"

That was it, I sat forward in my seat and scanned the horizon for a church like building, one missing a wall or two.

"Mum, I thought the Abbey was in the town, we are still in the countryside," said Olivia with a puzzled look on her face.

"It's in the town but high above it, we'll see the Abbey first before we reach the town," explained Mum.

"There it is!" I called out pointing to the Abbey ruins in the distance. It was black against the bright sky and it looked strange and ghostly, I could see why the story of Dracula was written here.

Olivia pulled at my arm, "Where? where is it?"

"There, can you see it now?" I pointed in it's direction but it had now disappeared.

"I can't see it," replied Olivia, "are you sure you saw it?"

"Yes, I did!" It gave me the shivers, had I seen it or was the chance of getting a pound putting pictures in my head? I sat back in my seat not wanting to show Olivia how confused I was.

"It's ok, you'll see it soon enough," said Dad "Gran and Grandad's holiday cottage is just below the Abbey."

"But you said the cottage was right by the beach Dad!" Olivia looked puzzled again.

"It is!" said Dad.

I was really looking forward to this holiday. It was Gran and Grandad's favourite holiday place and we were going to spend a whole week with them. Aunty

Sarah, Uncle John, Sam and Emma were also going to be there. Sam and Emma are our cousins, they're younger than me and Olivia but are still great fun. Sam loves football and Emma's just a baby but she's so cute.

We're staying with Gran and Grandad. Sam and Emma are in the next cottage with their Mum and Dad and Uncle James and Aunty Zoë. I was sure this was going to be a great holiday.

I turned to look out of the window to find that the countryside had been replaced by row after row of houses. Within a few minutes we were right in the middle of the town. The noise from hundreds of seagulls told us we were now near the harbour. And there it was on our left full of small boats and fishing trawlers. "Look Olivia that bridge is a swing bridge, Grandad told me about it."

"What does that mean?" asked Olivia.

"It means that the whole bridge swings around to let the larger boats through. The other side of that bridge leads to the sea."

"Wow, are we going over it Dad?"

"No not this time we are turning up this road here." And at that Dad drove up a very narrow but busy road. It was buzzing with holiday makers sauntering up the middle of the cobbled street not realising that cars were able to use it for access to the holiday cottages at the end of it.

The street was lined with very old shops and cafes. I smiled at the people as we passed but very few smiled back, we were upsetting their sauntering. I overheard one person say 'they can't drive up here they must be lost.'

Still crawling through the people we then turned right up a steep bend in the road. Ahead of us were stone steps reaching high up the side of the hill. Then at the right of the steps was a road which was steeper even than the steps themselves.

"No way Dad, there is no way we can drive up there!" shouted Olivia.

Dad laughed, "It's ok Olivia, that's not the road, once we get past these people you'll see the road bends to our left."

We continued crawling forward over the cobbles and to the left of the steps. The shops disappeared and all that was left were old buildings on each side of us. Finally we could see the end of them and the road ahead. Dad turned into a small parking area where he pulled in tight behind Grandad's car.

At last we were able to get out and stretch our legs, it had been a long journey.

As we loaded ourselves up with bags and cases, Grandad turned up to help. Just across from us was the sea, Olivia and me just stood there looking out across the bay. We were high above the beach and half way up the cliff face. It was an amazing view, but what was more amazing was that it had even left Olivia speechless. (if you knew Olivia, then you'd know that this didn't happen very often!) The air smelt salty and now we were away from the holiday makers all we could hear were the sea gulls' cries and the waves crashing against the stone pier below. We walked back down the street we had come up, then out from one of the doorways Gran appeared. She ran towards us, her arms open wide and a broad smile across her face. Whenever I saw her I couldn't help but smile to myself, she was more of a kid than we were. She was now bouncing up and down with excitement. Grandad handed her a box with Digger's food and bedding in. This should've slowed her down, but it didn't. Grandad winked at me whispering that she'd been like it all morning waiting for us.

Digger, our dog, ran back and forwards with excitement not knowing who to go to first. Finally Grandad won the privilege.

We went inside the cottage, it had low ceilings. Through the kitchen were steps down to the lounge and dining area. It was just one large room from the front of the cottage to the back. Patio doors then lead onto the balcony overlooking the sea and beach. We were still high up.

Mum said, "First things first, you need to take your bags up to the bedroom." I ignored her hoping she wouldn't ask us again.

We both stood there looking out to sea when Dad shouted. "Christopher, Olivia, did you hear what your Mum said?" We couldn't ignore it this time by the tone of dad's voice I knew he meant business.

We reluctantly pulled ourselves away from the view and went back inside. Grandad picked up a case and a couple of bags and said, "Follow me, but grab some bags on the way."

We followed him up a spiral staircase, it was great, it felt like we were going up a lighthouse. However it consisted of only ten creaky steps before reaching the bedroom. The room was large with a double bed and two single ones.

Grandad pointed to the single beds, "Those are yours, fight amongst yourselves as to which one you want, the double is Mum and Dad's," then he left us to decide.

We both dropped everything and rushed over to the window. Yes, we were still overlooking the bay. We couldn't see the beach from here because we were up in the attic of the cottage. The window was set into the roof which prevented us from looking straight down, but it didn't stop us from having a good look at the bay. As the bay opened up to the sea two large walkways like stone piers reached out on each side like giant arms. They looked as if they were meant to join up in the middle but at the last minute had decided to leave a gap for the boats to come and go as they pleased. At the end of each arm were lighthouses, they looked like the arms were holding enormous rockets ready to be launched at the ends.

"Come on Olivia," I said "let's get our bags unpacked, the sooner it's done the sooner we'll be able to go down to the beach and explore."

Within five minutes we were back on the balcony standing by the rail. Grandad called to us, "I guess you want to go down to the beach?"

"Yes Grandad, but how do we get down there, do we have to go back up to the car park."

"You can go that way, but there is an easier way, follow me." Grandad stepped out onto the balcony with us, he then turned left at the end of the balcony and disappeared down some wooden steps. We had been so busy looking out across the bay we hadn't noticed them. The steps lead down onto a lower part of the terraced garden and then across a small wooden bridge. Then down some stone steps. Half way down they sank into the garden, the stone walls closed in around us taking us into the dark and leading us to a gate which opened onto the beach. This was great, our own entrance to the beach.

"Chris! Olivia!" I turned to see who was shouting our names. It was Sam, he came running down the steps with Uncle John following close behind.

"Isn't it great, we turned up about an hour ago." exclaimed Sam.

"Where are you stopping Sam, we're with Gran and Grandad right at the top of these steps." As I looked up Aunty Sarah was coming towards us with Emma in her arms.

"We're just next door to you." Sam explained pointing to another balcony. "Uncle James and Aunty Zoë are staying with us."

The three of us started running down to the sea until we heard Aunty Sarah call out for us to stop Emma. As soon as Aunty Sarah had put her down on the beach she was off running in our direction trying to catch up with us. She was only eighteen months old but that didn't seem to stop her, she always joined in with us not realising she was too young for some games.

Sam her brother was six years old and Olivia my sister is seven. I am the eldest, twelve, which makes me responsible for all of them, including Emma who seems to fear nothing and no-one. She is the hardest to control.

As she ran towards us, laughing and screaming out loud with excitement, we got ourselves ready to catch her. With one last scream she crashed into Sam sending him flat on his back. Olivia and me helped them both to their feet and dusted the sand from their clothes. Olivia and Sam took hold of Emma's hands and we continued down to the waters edge.

Aunty Sarah soon caught up with us, Emma thought this was a great game and decided to run from her Mummy giggling as she did. Both Sam and Olivia tried to hold on to her but she took them by surprise and broke free. Before we knew it she was in the water with all of us following her. My jeans and trainers were soaked, Sam and Olivia had shorts and sandals on so they were ok and as for Emma, she didn't care about anything, she was just having the time of her life. After a short time of play Emma allowed us to lead her back up the beach where Uncle John had laid out a big rug for us all to sit on.

Aunty Sarah sat down next to Emma and slipped off Emma's wet clothes. Emma tried to reach out for the plates of food that Gran and Grandad were placing on the centre of the rug. "You best tuck in while there's still some left," said Gran as she struggled to hold onto a plate that Emma had decided to help Gran with.

After we had our fill, Uncle James and Aunty Zoë suggested Sam, Olivia and me go with them for a walk along the pier.

Gran and Grandad said they were going to take Emma and Digger for a walk in the hope that Emma would have a well needed sleep.

My jeans were still wet but it didn't matter, I didn't want to waste anymore time than was necessary.

The five of us headed back to the cottage and out onto the road to get to the pier. We had to go back up to the car park and down a steep concrete path to get to the start of the pier.

There were huge boulders and rocks on either side of the walkway. Sam shouted to Uncle James that he had found some dinosaur footprints. Uncle James gave nothing away, the footprints were obviously man-made for the tourists. Olivia was about to say something until she saw me shake my head and guessed that for Sam's benefit we were not to spoil his find.

Sam was engrossed in trying to work out what dinosaur could have made the prints and then announced, "Hang on a minute, these footprints are on the concrete walkway as well as the rocks! They can't be real, dinosaurs died before people lived and concrete is made by people."

We carried on walking up onto the pier while Sam chatted to Aunty Zoë about dinosaurs. Sam was fascinated by dinosaurs, so much that he knew more about them than all of us put together.

The pier was nothing like the piers you see at most holiday places, to start with there were no railings. It was a very wide stone built causeway stretching out to sea with steep sloping sides. As we walked further out I noticed that on the side of the pier that faced the sea the waves were rough and choppy, while on the side that faced the land the sea was so much calmer. Uncle James explained that the pier acted as a breakwater, breaking up the waves and stopping the force of them from smashing against the cliffs, something I hadn't thought about until now. But seeing the force of the waves at close hand I could understand how destructive the sea could be. As we neared the end of the pier you could see it wasn't straight at all. At the lighthouse there was a gap between the pier and another part of the pier which was made of wood. There had once been a bridge there, it was easy to see where it had stood. The lighthouse looked huge and yet it was smaller than the one on the opposite pier. Uncle James explained that from time to time the lighthouse on the other side was opened up for visitors and that the view from the top was fantastic. We looked back to see if we could see Mum and Dad, we could, they were the ones frantically waving to us. It was time to head back.

There were fewer people on this pier compared with the one on the other side. Maybe because the other had railings and was more accessible to the main part of the town, but to me this pier was far more interesting and exciting.

As we returned to the path which lead up to the road I hadn't seen that there was another path leading to the beach. "Why didn't we come up that way Uncle James?" I asked.

"Didn't you notice? the tide was in blocking our way. It's now going out so we can go down that way, but be careful."

It was great, we could walk straight down onto the beach. It was lined on each side with large boulders. The ramp itself was slimy at the bottom where the sea had covered it at high tide. Uncle James helped Olivia and Aunty Zoë down the ramp, past the slime. Sam and me decided to miss the slime by climbing over the boulders.

Dad and Mum were relaxing on the balcony with Gran and Grandad, "Well how was it?" asked Dad.

"It was great, I can't wait to go out there again." I replied.

Sam told Gran and Grandad about the footprints and how they couldn't be the real thing. Grandad said, "well if it's dinosaurs you want you'll have to wait until the tide goes out a little more. That's the best time to go looking for fossils."

Gran added, "yes, that's my favourite time but it's going to be a while yet before that happens. Instead would you like to go to the museum to see what kind of dinosaurs actually lived here?"

"Yes please Gran," said Sam excitedly.

"What else is there Gran?" asked Olivia.

"You know I'm not sure, I've never been there myself, but it won't all be about dinosaurs, some I'm sure will be about the people who lived here that became famous, like Captain Cook, pirates and er..."

That was it, before Gran could finish what she was saying we were all at the door ready to go. "Come on Grandad," said Olivia. Gran and Grandad followed leaving Mum and Dad relaxing. Digger was under the table trying to get some peace.

CHAPTER 2

Stepping into the past

Down the cobbled street we went, with Gran calling "wait for us!" At the Abbey steps we stopped to let Gran and Grandad catch up. We carried on through the narrow streets and crowds. Finally at the main road we headed for the swing bridge.

"Look the bridge is closed," said Sam.

"Come on lets get closer" said Grandad.

There were gates across the road stopping people and cars, a bit like a railway crossing. As we got closer we saw large boats passing close by heading for the sea, their tall masts reaching for the sky. We could see right down onto their decks. The crews were busy with lobster pots, nets and the rigging. Most were obviously fishing boats, others just for the tourists. But the best bit was when the bridge started to move. It swung round back into position joining the road up again. It was amazing to think that this middle section of the bridge with all its weight could move so smoothly. The gates were opened and the people flooded across the bridge. The cars were held back by traffic lights until everyone was safely across.

We carried on through the town which followed the path of the estuary. Within minutes we spotted the masts of a tall sailing ship, this was no ordinary ship! It looked like an old pirate ship and was painted black and a yellowy gold and had three tall masts.

Grandad said "Let's go see it up close."

It was called 'The Grand Turk'. We found out that it had been used in the TV series 'Hornblower' and was here in Whitby for the summer, as an attraction. We decided to board it and look round. A man in a pirate's costume introduced himself as the Captain. He told us about the days of old, what the sailors did and how they lived. We followed him through the ship as he pointed out all the wondrous things about life on board. However the food was another thing!

And if you fell ill, which was quite common because of the poor food, the likelihood of you recovering was very remote. You would more or less end up as shark food!

Time was getting on, we needed to make our way to the museum before it closed for the day.

Finally we reached it, but we were all feeling a bit tired and wished we'd left it for another day. But as Gran said, "we're here now so we might as well go in and see what there is."

Once inside, the place was so much cooler and darker. My eyes had to adjust to the difference between the brilliant sunshine outside and the darkened rooms inside.

At this point we all seemed to split up into groups. Gran went off to check out dinosaur fossils with Sam and Grandad told me and Olivia about Captain Cook who was a great traveller. Then something caught my eye, it was a mummified hand. It looked gruesome. Olivia was caught up with the adventures of Captain Cook so it made it easy for me to slip away to investigate the hand more closely.

The story behind the 'Hand of Glory' as it was named, was that it had probably come from the body of a hanged thief. Apparently the hand was mummified with fat rendered from the dead man's body. It was then pickled in a special way to preserve it. It was used by thieves who believed it had magical powers. Before entering a house they planned to burgle, they would place a candle between the hand's fingers or even light one of the fingers itself. This they believed would ensure the people in the house would remain asleep, but it did not work on those still awake.

I carried on looking around but couldn't help thinking about the hand. As we caught up with one another I had to show them all the HAND OF GLORY.

"Is it real?" asked Olivia.

"It's not turned into rock like the fossils we've been looking at, has it Gran?" said Sam looking serious.

"It must be real or it wouldn't be here, but you're right Sam it hasn't turned to stone so it can't be millions of years old, it may only be hundreds of years old or less." answered Gran looking even closer at it through the glass.

"What happened to the rest of the man?" asked Olivia.

Before I could answer one of the museum attendants turned up and asked us very nicely if we could make our way to the exit as it was closing time. Gran and Grandad apologised and thanked them for their patience and we left.

Back at the cottage we told everyone about the ship and the museum. Sam went into detail about all the different dinosaurs he'd seen and told us where they had been found and by whom. I told Dad and

Uncle James about the Hand of Glory while Olivia was asking Grandad when he was going to take her to see the Abbey.

After dinner we all went out on to the beach to look for fossils. Gran showed us what to look for and where to find them. There was a definite line of black pebbles where the waves had washed them up. It was along this line that the best fossils were to be found. Ammonites were coiled shelled animals that lived in the sea millions of years ago, it was hard but not impossible to find these. More often than not we were coming across parts of them. It was still a good feeling finding even the small bits.

Emma however found chasing Digger was far more exciting, at least it was one way of keeping her away from the water. All we had to do was call Digger back when he was heading that way. Poor Digger, Emma loved him so much. Although Digger, like so many dogs, loved the attention, Emma was very generous with her affections, it was often too much for him to bare.

Still as Dad said, "He won't need much walking this week with Emma on hand."

"And I think Emma will sleep well tonight" said Aunty Sarah as she watched Emma closely.

It was still light when the grown-ups left us on the beach, still hunting for fossils. Uncle John was carrying Emma who was crying and fighting him every step of the way up to the cottage. We didn't want to go in but we had had enough searching in the sand. We sat on some rocks and looked through our finds.

We had collected lots of bits of ammonites and some long thin pencil like stones that had a pointed end. Gran had told us these were belemnites, from a squid type creature. We had also found parts of broken white clay pipes. Olivia had the best one measuring at least eight centimetres. "Do you think it belonged to a pirate?" she questioned.

"I don't know, it could have." I paused in thought, "it would be good if it did."

Sam added, "A lot of fishermen smoked pipes like these, it could have been a fisherman."

"Yes I know, but I'd like to believe that it belonged to a pirate," answered Olivia, fingering it as she said it.

"Grandad said even women smoked pipes in those days," I explained "but like you, I'd like to think that it was used by a pirate."

"Chris tell us about that hand, where did it come from and whose was it?" asked Sam.

"Yes Chris, you were going to tell us and then we had to leave. Go on tell us the story behind the hand?"

"Ok then but it is a bit scary," I told them everything I could remember about the 'Hand of Glory'. And the way in which it was used by thieves to ensure that the people in the house, that they were about to burgle, remained asleep. I also added a lot of grim detail to the story which seemed ok until it got darker, then even I felt a bit scared as the noise of the birds appeared to get louder and louder. But I didn't let on.

"I think it's time we went up to the cottage Chris, it's got a bit spooky and creepy, don't you think?" said Olivia.

"Yes I think it's time Olivia, how about you Sam?"

"Oh yes, I'm not going to stay down here on my own."

So we headed up the steps through the terraced gardens to Sam's cottage and knocked on the patio windows. Aunty Sarah slid open the door, "Shh, Emma is sleeping, how did you get on? What did you find?"

We stood there and just looked at each other. Then Sam said, "We've left them at the bottom of the steps."

"Don't worry Sam, we'll go back and get them, we'll keep them until morning." I said, and he smiled and made his way into the cottage.

As we turned to leave, Olivia looked at me in disbelief, "You are joking aren't you Chris, I'm not going back down there again it's pitch black now!"

"Well we can't let him down and I'm not going down there on my own!"

Just then, we heard a noise! It was Dad. "At last,

I was just coming to get you two." We told him we had left our finds on the beach and were just about to go back for them. "Go on then I'll watch you from here."

"No way Dad, I'm not going down there in the dark, Chris will have to do it on his own!"

"I'm not going on my own, if I do I'll just bring mine and Sam's up!"

"Now you can just stop there, we'll all go down but first of all Chris go get the torch from inside, that way if anything is going to creep up on us we will see it coming." said Dad with a smirk.

"Oh Dad!" said Olivia as she thumped him hard in his side.

I returned with the torch and we headed back down the steps. "There's nothing to be frightened of you know." said Dad half smiling and half laughing.

We made our way back to the beach, picked up our finds and headed back. Our first day had been great.

CHAPTER 3

Graves

The next morning Olivia and me were up early, in fact we were the first ones up. Everyone else was in bed.

We had breakfast outside on the balcony, Olivia thought it would be a good idea to throw the remains of her toast out to the sea gulls. What a big mistake! They screamed and screeched as they swooped to get as close as possible to the flying food. But it didn't stop there, fights broke out between the desperate gulls. They started to swoop at each other and for those on the gardens below, a frenzy of flapping and pecking at each other started. All desperate for the few crumbs that had made it to the ground.

We backed in through the patio doors to escape the gulls, closing them out as we went. It was great to watch them so close up as they landed on the table in search for more food. They were larger than I'd expected!

"What have you two been up to?" asked Grandad who had suddenly appeared from nowhere.

"We were feeding the gulls Grandad, when it all got out of hand," said Olivia.

"What do you mean we, I had nothing to do with it!" I said.

"It's ok, gulls don't have manners, I think you've got that message now," replied Grandad, putting a stop to our argument.

"Yes, we sure have, but it was cool to see them so close up." Grandad carried on making coffee for Gran, who was still in bed. "We're going down to the beach Grandad to play some footie, do you think Sam will be up yet?"

"Well, with those gulls still watching for you, you'd better go out the front door and down by the pier. As for Sam, yes, I reckon he'll be ready and waiting, but don't go without his fossils. Your Dad told us about last night and how after all your hard searching you forgot them." He smiled at us as he unlocked the front door. "Just be careful, I'll be keeping an eye on you from the window."

Olivia grabbed the bag and I grabbed the football. Sam was already up waiting for us but expected to go via the steps. We told him all about the gulls as we made our way down to the beach.

Once on the beach we started to kick the ball about, just to warm up. A little further up the beach were two other boys playing footie and some people walking at the edge of the water. We were soon into our game when Dad turned up with Digger.

"What's the score?" shouted Dad as he approached.

"We're just taking it in turn to score goals, but no one's managed it yet."

"There's not enough of you to have a good kick about, why don't you join up with those two lads up there," said Dad pointing in the direction of the two boys we'd noticed earlier. Then Dad carried on past us without waiting for an answer.

I wasn't sure what to say and neither did Sam or Olivia by the looks on their faces. I guessed they were thinking the same as me, 'Were they going to be ok? were they going to mix in with us? or was this going to be a bad move?'

We watched as Dad walked nearer to the boys then stopped. They were kicking their ball to one another, then they stopped and looked over to Dad. Dad was now talking to them and pointing in our direction. It was all too embarrassing, I dropped the ball on my foot and kicked it into the air. Next thing Sam and Olivia started to call for me to kick the ball in their direction. Within minutes the two boys had joined in the game. We didn't have to stop and sort out who was doing what, we just carried on enjoying the kick about.

After quite a while Gran and Grandad walked down the steps towards us, "We're going up to the Abbey," said Gran, "anyone interested in coming with us?"

"Yes, I am Gran," shouted Olivia with excitement.

"What about the rest of you?" said Grandad.

"We were right in the middle of a game, can't it wait till later Grandad?" said Sam.

"Well the game can't carry on for long, look." Grandad pointed to the water's edge. "The tide is about to come in. You can always make arrangements to meet up with your new friends later." said Grandad then added "Why don't they join us? if it's ok with their parents."

"That would be great," said Olivia.

"Sounds good to us, we're stopping in that cottage up there, we'll just go and ask them." said the older lad.

"That's right next to us," said Sam, "we'll wait here for you."

They climbed the steps up to their cottage, just a little further along from ours. Within minutes their Dad made his way down to us. Grandad and Gran chatted for a while with him, then nodded some kind of agreement.

"By the way what's your names?" asked Gran.

"I'm Jack and this is my brother Joey." said the older lad in reply.

As we set off we introduced ourselves and talked on the way. We went along the beach and up through an alley way at the opposite side of the cottages. This place was full of surprises! We came out onto the cobbled street near the bottom of the Abbey steps. I'd been looking forward to seeing the Abbey, Grandad had told me all about it and he had taken lots of photos, some in the dark which made it look very eerie indeed.

We started counting the steps but Grandad kept putting us off by saying a different number to what we were saying so we gave up. Us older ones found it funny but Olivia and Sam told Grandad off for spoiling their efforts. Gran joined in and scolded Grandad who then said he was sorry and that he wouldn't do it again. As soon as Gran headed off, leading the way up the steps with Olivia and Sam, Grandad smiled at us with a cheeky grin, I returned the smile knowing that Grandad liked to cause trouble from time to time. 'Another big kid!'

At the top was a church and graveyard.

"Is this it Gran?" asked Olivia.

"No this is Saint Mary's church, the Abbey is behind the graveyard." replied Gran, pointing to the far end where a high stone wall stood.

The graves were old and very worn with the weather and sea air. It was hard to read the gravestones and some were so badly affected by erosion that there was nothing left to read. Neither did they stand up straight, they were crooked having sunk down into the ground.

"Come on sit over here, I've got lunch for you all," said Gran as she pulled foil wrapped sandwiches out from her bag.

The church was open so after we'd finished eating we all walked through the doors to have a look inside.

All the pews were boxed in with doors at the ends. "Why are they like that Grandad?" I asked.

"Well it's to keep everyone in so that the vicar can deliver his sermon without anyone escaping," explained Grandad with a smile.

At that he received a prod in the side from Gran. "Now tell them the real facts and behave yourself!"

"Oh alright," said Grandad grinning and then told us about why the pews were the way they were. "Firstly, they were designed this way to keep the different classes separate and families together.

The front ones were mainly for the gentry and the ones at the back were for the simple fishermen. The gentry would make theirs comfortable with cushions and blankets, while the poor folk sat on the bare wooden seats."

"Grandad someone's been scratching the shape of a boat here," said Sam pointing to the back of a pew.

"Let's see," I said as I bent down to see where Sam was pointing. Sure enough there it was, but it wasn't recent, it had been painted over and not just once. "It looks very old Grandad."

"Yes it's graffiti," he said

"Graffiti!" said Olivia.

"Yes, there is more upstairs but it's closed off to the public," Grandad stepped closer to us and in a whisper said, "I still think they were so bored with the sermons that they occupied themselves by carving boats like this one." We all smiled then went off to look for more interesting things.

"Did pirates come to this church Grandad?" asked Sam.

"Well I'm not sure, but if they did visit the town I don't think they would let anyone know they were pirates. They'd be arrested and imprisoned until their trial and then hanged."

"So Grandad do you reckon that there were pirates here in Whitby?" said Olivia.

"Yes, I reckon there must have been as well as smugglers and thieves. Like the one's that used the 'Hand of Glory', why don't you tell Jack and Joey about that Chris."

So I told them the story, as we made our way out of the church and through the graveyard.

I continued the story as we entered the grounds of what looked like an old manor house. Sam and Olivia were up ahead of us with Gran and Grandad, when I heard a scream! It was Emma, she was obviously glad to see us.

"Chris, catch her will you!" shouted Aunty Sarah.

She ran straight into my arms giggling as she did. "This is Emma my cousin," I explained.

"Pleased to meet you," said Jack smiling at Emma.

"She's cute," said Joey.

"I'm glad you like her, it's very hard to escape from her, she even plays football," I said smiling. I put her down and we walked into the building with Aunty Sarah and Uncle John.

"Oh great a family gathering, but where's Peter and Vicky?" said Gran.

"They've gone into town shopping," answered Aunty Sarah.

Looking round, this large building had a very modern interior. We were each given a personal cassette player to listen to explaining the history of the Abbey. But first we were told to enjoy the rest of the activities in the building before going into the grounds of the Abbey.

We went upstairs where there were video screens and different activities, along with display cabinets with lots of interesting objects which had been found in the grounds of the Abbey.

Some of the information was about the building we were in. The surprise was that it was only the front of the building that was left and that it was a shell before they built the new interior.

Outside stood what was left of the Abbey, it was impressive! We all wandered off in different directions. Grandad busied himself taking photos, Gran went off with Olivia into the heart of the ruins and Sam and Emma ran circles round Aunty Sarah and Uncle John.

I lost sight of Jack and Joey for a while and then I heard my name called.

"Over here Chris," said Jack, "come and see this grave!"

Both Jack and Joey were stood by an empty stone coffin which was sunk into the ground. It was small and I wondered who had been buried there.

Jack, Joey and me stuck together as we carried on looking at the ruins and listening to the information tape. This was going to be a bit of a strange holiday, so far all I'd come across was fossilized remains of dead animals, a mummified hand and graves, some of which were missing their dead bodies. No wonder the Dracula story was written here!

As we all made our way back through the graveyard we were stopped at the top of the steps by Olivia and Sam.

"Now we want you all to keep quiet while we count the steps on our way down," said Olivia.

"Yes especially you Grandad," added Sam.

We stood back and let Sam and Olivia set off first. Right at the top of the steps was a large cross, I hadn't noticed it when we came up. It was stone with intricate designs and writings. Yet another reminder of death and the past. History was just another subject at school, but now it was all around me and I quite liked it.

At the bottom of the steps we caught up with Sam and Olivia. "Well how many steps?"

"One hundred and ninety nine steps" said Sam.

"Yes that's right, we were careful to count every step on the way down. But it does sound wrong somehow." added Olivia.

"Why's that?" said Grandad.

"Well it's an odd number, you'd think they'd make sure it rounded up to two hundred." said Olivia.

"Well I don't know how they planned it but you are spot on with your count," said Grandad, holding the guide book.

"Come on, let's get back and see what the others have been up to." said Gran as she headed for the cottage.

CHAPTER 4

Footie

The tide had retreated leaving the beach clear and flat. That was our chance to play some serious football.

It wasn't that easy playing on wet sand, which made it all the more interesting. Sam, Olivia and me were well ahead at half time with four goals to one. Jack and Joey were not happy and grumbled all the time. However when we switched ends it was hard to readjust to the slope of the pitch. In addition to that was the brilliant sunlight blinding us as we tried to see the goal area. I realised that Jack and Joey had had good reason to grumble.

We sat down to talk through these problems. Finally we agreed to play with just one goal, which would be against the wall of the terraced garden and that we would take it in turns to be in goal. That meant two in each team.

This time the game worked, although it still wasn't easy now that the sand was drying out and that all the goal shooting was up hill.

All that evening was ours, the adults were just chilling out and doing their own thing. Gran and Grandad were sat on the balcony watching and waving from time to time.

Suddenly, out of nowhere Digger ran right across my path and sent me flying. Before I could say anything I heard Aunty Sarah shout, "Look out!"

I rolled over onto my back in order to sit up thinking she was a bit late with her warning, when I was hit again, this time while I was still down.

It was Emma who was lying across my chest. Jack came to my rescue, lifting Emma up in his arms while Sam helped me to my feet.

She was unhurt and in a hurry to get free to continue her mission to catch Digger.

"Digger, come here!" shouted Olivia. Digger responded but took his time to return with his ears and head down.

"Sorry about that Chris, are you ok?" asked Aunty Sarah as she struggled to take hold of Emma.

"I'm fine," I dusted the sand from my clothes.

Olivia held onto Digger's collar as Emma was allowed once again to take advantage of his capture and patted him while chattering away to him.

"Let's call it a day and play with Emma," said Olivia.

"That's ok with me," said Jack.

"It looks as if it'll be fun," added Joey.

"Well, it doesn't mean we have to stop playing football, Emma loves the game." said Sam.

"Come on then, whose side is she going on?" I asked.

"Well she won't stick to a team, we'll just have to play around her, allowing her to kick the ball from time to time," explained Sam.

"Let's give it a try," I picked up the ball and gently kicked it in Emma's direction.

It worked. She ran around us as we kicked the ball to each other giving her the chance to take it from us whenever she got close. When we scored a goal, it didn't matter which side scored, Emma's arms would fly up into the air and she'd scream with delight, "Goal!"

Finally it was time to call it a day, Mum waved to us to come up. We'd had a great time even with Emma's participation.

"We'll see you later Chris!" called Jack.

"Yes, we'll meet you on the beach by the gate."

We sat round the table tucking into a late supper of pizzas and pasta.

"What are you doing after this Chris?" asked Gran.

"Back out playing footie Gran, why?"

"Well I need you to give me a hand with something."

"Will it take long, I've got the guys meeting us?"

"Well they could help too," she replied

"With what Gran?" she had me puzzled.

"When you've finished you and Olivia can come up to the car with me."

Olivia looked at me wondering what Gran was going on about, then it suddenly struck me-Grandad's birthday!

"I'm ready when you are Gran, come on Olivia let's go."

Olivia still didn't get it even after all the plotting Mum and Dad had been up to, hiding Grandad's present and cards.

Gran lead the way up to the car park while I whispered to Olivia that I thought it was about Grandad's birthday.

In the car park Gran went to Aunty Sarah's car. "Look it's Grandad's birthday tomorrow."

I butted in looking straight at Olivia "Told you that was it."

Gran continued, "Yes but the real secret is that we are going to have a party. A pirates party!"

"Wow, that sounds great Gran," said Olivia.

"So tonight I need you to sort out your outfits. Look!" she said as she opened the boot of the car. "We've brought a load of bits and pieces that might help. I want you to take them all to Aunty Sarah's cottage and sort out your outfits."

"When's the party Gran?" I asked.

"Tomorrow afternoon. Oh and you can invite your new friends and their Mum and Dad."

"That's great."

"Come on then Chris let's get this lot down to Aunty Sarah's." said Olivia.

"Remember, it's going to be a surprise, so not a word to Grandad!"

"It's safe with us Gran." I called as we ran to Aunty Sarah's with a large bag in each hand.

Aunty Sarah and Mum helped us all to pick the things needed to make up our outfits. There were leather belts, scarves, T-shirts and even some eye patches.

"Where's the captain's hat?" asked Sam.

"Ah, that be for the Captain, whose birthday it be the morrow," said Aunty Sarah trying to sound like a pirate.

"Oh you mean Grandad!" replied Sam a little disappointed that he couldn't be captain.

Then Olivia said, "We need to meet up with Jack and Joey and let them know what's happening tomorrow. They'll need to sort out their outfits too."

"Can I come too?" said Sam as we made our way to the balcony.

"Go on then but just for half an hour," said Aunty Sarah.

"Yes!" shouted Sam, his arms waving in the air as though he'd scored the goal of a life time.

We were making our way down the steps when we heard Emma cry out "Sam!" followed by crying.

"She'll get over it" said Sam, "she doesn't understand that she's just too young to join us older ones."

Jack and Joey were waiting for us. We told them about the party and how they needed to sort out their outfits. A little later Dad called us in. It had been a full day.

CHAPTER 5

Party time

At breakfast we all sang happy birthday to Grandad, then handed over presents and cards. None of us mentioned the party. As he pulled out each card from it's envelope he smiled and then looked us full in the face and announced "I think we should have a party tonight." We looked at him wondering if he'd guessed what Gran had planned. "Yes," he said looking very thoughtful, then continued. "We'll have a pizza party, tonight. What do you think Gran?" he said as he turned to see what the answer would be. She was in the kitchen area bringing over Grandad's favourite, kippers.

"Well that sounds ok to me, what do you kids think?" as she said it she winked at us, behind his back.

"That sounds great Grandad," I said. "What about you Olivia?"

"Yes, do you want me to tell the others for you, we're going over to see Sam?" said Olivia.

"Yes, you spread the word and I'll organise the pizzas." replied Grandad.

"No Grandad, it's your birthday, let me organise the pizzas for you," said Gran.

At Sam's we told them about our close call and that Grandad was adamant on sorting out a party that evening.

"So are we having two parties?" said Sam.

"No Sam, one party is going to be enough to organise," said Aunty Sarah.

"Oh, that would have been great!" replied Sam now sounding down hearted.

"Remember Sam we have to make Grandad think that it is his pizza party that we are looking forward to," I said smiling in the hope of cheering him up.

"The pirates party is going to be so much better and just to let you into a secret Sam, Gran has already told us that we're having pizzas as well as lots more goodies," said Olivia.

"Great, pizzas are my favourite," said Sam.

"Come on, lets get out of everyone's way and head for the beach," said Uncle James.

Outside, Jack and Joey spotted us and came running over, "We can't stay we're going shopping for your Grandad's birthday present, said Jack, "we'll see you at the party."

"See you then," I carried on down to the water's edge following the others.

We all started looking for fossils, it was something to do as we waited for the preparations to start. Uncle James thought it wise for us to stay out of the way in case we slipped up and said something that would alert Grandad to the party. I also think he offered to be with us kids to avoid any jobs that needed doing. He's wise my Uncle James.

I was amazed at how many fossils we found. Each time we checked the beach it seemed to have that much more. Uncle James said it was because we were getting better at spotting them. I agreed.

We must have been searching for most of the morning without realising it because before we knew it Aunty Sarah was calling us to come up to their cottage.

It was time to get changed into our outfits.

I had an old pair of jeans cut off just below the knee and shredded. Also a white cotton shirt and a black leather waistcoat. Around my head I wore a red spotted bandana. Aunty Sarah started on the makeup while Gran handed me a large gold earring.

"You won't need shoes until later," said Gran.

"Why later? Are we going somewhere?" I asked.

"Oh yes, you can't have a pirate party without a treasure hunt," replied Gran.

"Yes!" shouted Sam and Olivia in unison.

Olivia wore red leggings cut and shredded like mine and a black and white striped top. Around her waist was a leather belt with a big brass buckle which hung loose. As well as the black bandana, she wore her hair in long thin plaits with beads and feathers in.

Sam's outfit was brown trousers, white satin shirt and brown waistcoat. He also had a belt with a sword attached. His bandana was brown to match his outfit and he wore an eye patch to complete the whole effect.

When I finally got to the mirror to checkout Aunty Sarah's skills as a makeup artist I was amazed. I had a marvellous scar all the way down my right cheek, it looked so real.

The three of us sat on the sofa waiting for the others to emerge from the bedrooms. We were all getting excited about the thought of the treasure hunt.

Then the door to one of the bedrooms opened and out came Mum, Aunty Sarah, Gran and Emma, all parading around us in their outfits.

Mum and Aunty Sarah were dressed very much like Olivia with their hair in plaits. Gran wore a battered hat and a long jacket with a stuffed parrot sitting on her shoulder. But the best of all was Emma who had red leggings on and a black and white striped T-shirt. On her head was a red bandana and Aunty Sarah had painted on her arm a tattoo. She also had a monkey on a lead.

"Where's Dad, Uncle John and Uncle James?" I asked.

"Well someone had to keep Grandad occupied while we got ready. They've taken him for a drink at the Black horse."

"So how are they going to get changed Gran?" said Sam.

"Well I'm going to phone Uncle Peter on his mobile to let him know we're ready and he's going to say there's a problem back here. He and Uncle John are going to come back and change followed by Grandad and Uncle James a little later."

"Do you think he'll cotton on to it when Dad and Uncle John leave?" I asked.

"I hope not." replied Gran. At that she picked up her phone and called Dad.

It wasn't long before Dad and Uncle John were back getting changed.

Back in Gran's cottage we started putting up jolly roger flags. The skull and crossbones made the place look like the captains cabin on board a pirates galleon. Gran and Mum busied themselves in the kitchen, or should I say galley, while Aunty Sarah helped us set the table with lots and lots of wonderful food. Instead of glasses we all had tankards including Emma and best of all it was all finger food, not a knife or fork in sight.

Digger was a white west highland terrier, but today even he had got into the act. Mum had painted a black patch over one eye and he was wearing a neckerchief around his neck.

With the balcony doors wide open and the sound of the seagulls it felt like we were truly on board a ship. Even though it was in the afternoon the room was quite dark. It was a long room starting at one end with the kitchen (galley) and a very small window, stretching through the dining area and into the lounge part before reaching the patio doors. We normally had the lights on but today it was dimly lit with candles.

A knock at the door stopped me from day dreaming any longer. Gran went to the door, it was Jack, Joey and their parents. For a moment we were lost in comparing outfits until another knock. Everyone went quiet.

Gran motioned for us all to get into place. We lined the room on both sides, then Gran opened the door.

We all shouted "SURPRISE!"

Grandad looked shocked, then started laughing at Gran's parrot. He edged his way past us not believing what he was seeing and commenting on our outfits.

"Come on Grandad you can't start enjoying the party until you get into your outfit," said Gran pulling at his arm.

"I don't think I've got anything that will match this lot," answered Grandad as he looked around the room.

"Just take yourself in there, it's all waiting for you," said Gran pointing to the bedroom.

Moments later Grandad emerged in a long green coat with gold braid and gold buttons down the front and black pants. He had a white satin shirt and best of all was his battered captain's hat, under which he wore a green bandana.

Grandad always wore a ruff stubbly beard, so he looked the part, a real pirate if ever there was one.

Everyone cheered followed by the Happy Birthday song that everyone dreads.

"Come on then me hearties, let's tuck into this fine feast before us." said Grandad in his attempt to sound hard and loud.

We all tucked into the food and enjoyed the fun of being in character. There were lots of 'shiver me timbers' and talk about 'doubloons' buried close by.

Digger was finding his own treasure and storing it under the table. Emma just dropped what she didn't want and Digger took the opportunity to hide it where feet couldn't trample it.

Amidst all the noise Emma finally fell asleep, this was what Gran was waiting for.

"Right we've all 'eard the tale about Spanish Gold and that it's been said that it's somewhere in these parts. So we'll 'ave no mutiny, we'll 'ave to all work together to find it. Some of us 'ave to stay behind to guard the ship, but we'll be watching. Polly my parrot can still fly high enough to see what ya all up to. So get out there on that beach and look for clues that will lead you to the treasure." Gran pointed out to sea with an air of authority.

We all scurried out of the patio doors and down the steps excited at the prospect of finding the treasure. We left Gran and Aunty Sarah behind along with Emma who was sound asleep and Digger who was still under the table with his own treasure.

CHAPTER 6

In search of treasure

Grandad took charge and told everyone to look for something unusual, the kind of something that might lead to a map.

We all went off in small groups and in different directions. People on the beach stopped to look at us and small children pointed, shouting to their mums and dads to look at the pirates.

It didn't matter to us, we were enjoying ourselves. Our outfits had given us boldness, we were fearless.

Anyone laughing would have to walk the plank. We were on a mission to find the treasure!

"Here, I've found a bottle!" shouted Olivia. We all ran to the edge of the sea where she stood with what looked like a very old ale bottle. Inside was a piece of paper rolled up tightly.

The bottle passed from person to person, or should I say pirate to pirate in an effort to shake the scroll out of the bottle. Someone shouted, "Let's smash it!"

But the Captain took charge of the bottle and said "It be a foolish thing to do that. We might draw attention to ourselves doing such a terrible thing as that. No we will 'ave to find the one of us who 'as the nimblest fingers among us."

Olivia held her hand up and said, "Would that be me captain?"

"'Ere do ya best," said the Captain as he handed over the bottle to Olivia.

Within seconds the scroll was out and being unrolled carefully. It was damp and the ink had run but we could still make out the words.

BEASTS OF OLD WALKED THIS WAY

We kept repeating it until Sam said that it might be to do with dinosaurs and the footprints that we had seen up on the pier.

We headed up the beach towards the pier and climbed the slope to where we had first seen the footprints.

"Look around the rocks me hearties," ordered Captain Grandad.

This time it was Jack who pulled out another piece of paper from between two rocks. It read:

ON THE WAY TO 199 VISIT THE FISH WHO IS AFTER MY TREASURE

"What does that mean?" said Joey.

"Well the 199 must be the steps," said Olivia, "we counted them yesterday."

"Well let's make our way there and we might be able to work out the rest of the clue," said Dad.

We made our way up the hill to the top where it met the cobbled road and car park.

"Of course, the Captain's favourite breakfast," called out Dad.

"What toast?" said Grandad with a confused look on his face.

"No what did you have this morning?"

Grandad stood there thinking, then I said, "Captain you had kippers this morning."

"Oh yes, but what's kippers got to do with the clue?" he said.

"Look Captain there's the shop where you bought them from. It's called 'Fortune's Kippers'.

"Fortune's Kippers, the fish that's after my treasure, of course, well let's get looking, another clue must be around here somewhere."

We crowded around the little shop looking for any clues. The Captain ended up in the shop explaining why we were there and hoping the owner might have an idea as to where the clue might be hiding. He was right.

"Yes I did see a lady this morning near the door to the smoking shed." said the owner.

"Thank you," replied Captain and then beckoned us over to the rear of the building. "It must be round 'ere me hearties."

This time I was the one who found it.

"What does it say?" asked Sam as he pushed his way between Dad and Uncle John.

I read it out aloud for all to hear.

ON LOOKING DOWN ON THE ENDEAVOUR,
ANOTHER CLUE YOU'LL FIND.............
HEPWORTH IS THE NAME.

There was silence as we stood there pondering on the meaning of the words. Then Mum said "the Endeavour it's a ship isn't it?"

"Yes, I think it was Captain Cook's ship!" said Joey.

"So where do we find it and do we continue going to the Abbey steps?" questioned Grandad.

I could tell we were all now getting serious about our search for the treasure. Our attempts at being pirates and sounding like them had all but gone. The clues were getting harder.

"Let's head towards the Abbey steps, it might help us to think." said Grandad as he lead the way.

As we approached the steps Mum shouted, "There it is, the Endeavour!"

Just at the start of the steps was a boat sat on top of a terraced garden area. I looked at the clue again. "It says 'on looking down on the Endeavour another clue you'll find'. That means we need to be above it to find the clue."

"Come on then, you lead the way Chris," said Mum.

As we climbed the steps we came to a point where we could all gather and look down on the boat. The boat was full of flowering plants and looked nothing like the Endeavour but that didn't matter. The name on it's side said Endeavour, that was enough for us. We were here to find the next clue.

"I can't see anything," said Grandad. "What else did it say Chris?"

I looked at the clue again. "It says 'on looking down on the Endeavour another clue you'll find........... Hepworth is the name'."

"So now we have to look for the name Hepworth. It could be a shop name or a street name. The main thing is that we should be able to see it from here," said Grandad.

We were still getting some funny looks, then a man asked if he could take our photo with his two little boys. Grandad agreed so we grouped together with the children stood in the centre of us. But it didn't stop there, more people asked to take our photos. A crowd was now gathering and some were asking questions. I heard Jack explaining to someone about the treasure hunt, it made me focus again, I had the clue.

CHAPTER 7

The lost clue

I rummaged in my pocket for it, but nothing, where was it! I looked on the ground where I stood, but still nothing!

"What's wrong Chris, can't you see we're having our photo taken!" said Dad impatient to get it over with and back to the serious task of looking for the treasure.

"I've lost the clue! I must have dropped it somewhere around here."

With that the photo call was forgotten and we all started looking at the ground in the hope of finding it.

Jack called out "What was the name again mentioned in the clue?"

"Hepworth." replied Jack's Dad.

"Well I think we've found the next clue. Look here, this grate has the name Hepworth on it and there's a note inside." announced Jack.

"Can you reach it?" asked Jack's Dad.

"No my fingers are too big." was the reply.

Sam pushed through to have a look, "I can get it." He tried to squeeze his fingers down into the grate but he just couldn't do it.

Mum then crouched down next to Sam, "Try this Sam." She gave him a lollipop stick. He pushed it through the bars of the grate and twisted it this way and that. Finally the corner of it popped up enough for Mum to pull it out in one piece.

Mum read it out to us.

CLIMB HIGHER TO THE CROSS, THREE STONES TO THE RIGHT IS YOUR NEXT CLUE

We all knew it meant we had to go to the top and look for a cross. At the top stood the tall stone cross, it had to be the one.

"Right then, me hearties, three stones to the right." said Grandad firmly. He was back in the role of the Captain again.

"What stones?" said Sam.

"I think it means these stones Sam." said Uncle John reassuring Sam and pointing to row after row of grave stones.

"There's too many rows, which third one along is it?" said Olivia, looking rather puzzled.

"Well if we all go to the third stone along in each row maybe we'll find one of them has a clue." said Grandad, having lost his pirate character again.

We all scanned the grave stones for some kind of

clue, but nothing! Then at the bottom of the one I was checking I noticed a jam jar with flowers in it. It seemed very strange, these graves were very old. I didn't think that other than close relatives anyone would put flowers on it and if they did I was sure they'd find something better than an old jam jar. I looked closer. There it was, a clue on the back of the jar.

"Grandad, I've found it!"

"Read it Chris."

LOOK TO TIME WITHOUT A WATCH, ROUND THE CLOCK YOU GO. MATTHEWS ON THE CORNER.

"Well that's easy," said Grandad. "I never wear a watch, I always look for a clock and there it is." We all looked to where he was pointing. "The Church clock, come on let's find Matthews."

At the clock we knew we had to go round it but which way? "Shall we split up and go round the church in different directions?"

"No Chris, I think it means we go round the church 'clock-wise', remember what Gran said 'work together'."

"Come on this way," said Dad. "Matthews has got to be a name on a grave stone, but which one.?"

Sure enough we came to a grave stone with the name Matthews on it and below was another jam jar with flowers in it.

Olivia picked it up and read out the next clue.

*KEEP THE CHURCH ON YOUR RIGHT, LOOK
BEHIND THE DEAD MEN RESTING.*

"Well we have the church to our right Grandad but what does it mean 'dead men resting'?" asked Olivia.

"Well Olivia I'm not sure myself." said Grandad.

"The best thing to do is move round the church until we see something that might be dead men resting," said Dad trying to be motivating.

"Well it worked before when we were looking for the Endeavour." said Sam in a positive voice.

I could tell Olivia was getting frustrated at this point, she was pulling at her hair. I wouldn't admit it myself but these clues were harder than I expected, not easy for the younger ones.

"You're right Sam, lets go and everyone keep your eyes open for anything that resembles 'dead men resting'." supported Uncle John.

We all followed but slowly, the heat was getting to us and I was hungry again. Sam was still eager to complete the hunt. I needed the pace to quicken up if I was to remain interested.

Only a little way on, there they were, three grave stones resting against the church wall. Under one was the next clue.

*DOWN TO TATE HILL, NOT UP, THE HARPIST
PLAYS THE TUNE.*

"Well at least we know which way is down, it's got to be back down the steps." Grandad lead the way, he was in his element. This was a great birthday for him and my thought of food had passed.

As we descended the steps we kept looking for a sign for Tate Hill. Just before we reached the bottom Aunty Zoë called out "There it is!"

It was a street sign next to some seating and in the middle was a statue. A harpist!

We all crowded round the statue looking for the clue. People sitting on the seating watched us with amusement. And then we found it, a leather pouch under his foot!

"This has got to be the final clue." said Jack. He pulled out another clue which read.

DOWN SANDSIDE, LOOK FOR THE FLAG FLYING.

"Sandside, that's got to be the beach!" said Joey excitedly.

"Yes but better than that, look, another street sign, 'Sandside' come on let's go." Jack was now leading the way. "Remember keep your eyes open for a 'flag flying'."

Sandside lead us onto a stone jetty. We all came together at the end of it still looking for a flag.

"Why did we have to go up to the church only to come back down?" said Olivia with her hands on her hips.

"That's a treasure hunt for you, it's meant to test you every step of the way. Anyway it wouldn't have been much of a treasure hunt if all we did was come straight here." explained Uncle James.

"Look, over there." said Grandad pointing to a shabby looking flag on the beach.

We jumped down onto the beach, helping Olivia and Sam as we did so. One by one we reached the flag attached to a weathered branch which looked as though it had been washed up on the beach at some point in time.

It was only then that we realised that we were just outside the gateway to the cottages.

"We've gone in a circle, we're back at the beginning." said Sam followed by an exhausted sigh.

"Let's not stop now we still have the treasure to find." said Grandad.

At the base of the flag pole, half buried in the sand was yet another note.

YOU'LL FIND MY TREASURE UNDER THE RING OF STONES.

CHAPTER 8

Lost treasure

We started scanning the beach for a circle of stones. This time we did split up. We spotted Aunty Sarah sat on a rug flicking through a magazine, pausing from time to time to check on Emma who was playing in the sand with some shells and stones.

Gran must have seen us from the cottage, she stepped onto the beach with a tray full of drinks. It was then that her smile suddenly changed to a look of disbelief. "Oh no!"

"What's wrong Gran?" I asked.

"Emma's playing with the stones that marked the treasure."

Everyone stopped in their tracks. Then Grandad in his pirate's voice ordered "Well then me hearties, what do you think we should do?"

"Lets dig!" shouted Sam.

"Yes" came the reply from all of us.

So that was it, we all started digging deep into the sand around Emma looking for the treasure.

It wasn't long before Digger himself joined us, he however was looking for his own type of treasure, bones!

Soon a shout went up from Jack. "I've found something!"

We all rushed over to see. "I've hit something solid" he said.

The sand was reluctant to let us see, it kept spilling back onto the hard surface. We all crowded round the hole and started scooping out the sand as quickly as we could. Underneath we found nothing but a black rock surface. "Oh no, I really thought I'd found it." sighed Jack.

"Not to worry, let's keep looking." said Uncle James, but we were all feeling disappointed.

Emma now thought that the hole was far more interesting than the stones. She made her way to the hole and sat down in it. We carried on digging holes all around where Aunty Sarah was sat but with no luck.

Just as we were ready to give up, Digger started barking. "Over here," shouted Joey. "Digger has found the treasure."

Sure enough Digger was scratching at a box set deep in the sand. We all scrambled round the hole for a look at the result of what had been an epic hunt. The box was dragged up out of the hole by Grandad. "Stand back me hearties or I'll cut ya livers out."

Grandad was back in character again and enjoying the power it gave him.

"Come on Grandad, we can't wait any longer." replied Sam.

"This be mutiny, be careful I don't make ye walk the plank." Added Grandad.

"Captain, there's more of us than there is of you." I said.

"Mmm, you have a point, I'll let Olivia open it. That way if it's disappointing then she will have to walk the plank." said Grandad.

Olivia pushed through to open the treasure box. The lid fell back to reveal a mountain of chocolate coins. We kids dived in leaving little for the adults, but they didn't seem to mind. It was obvious that they were glad, at last, to sit down and relax.

It wasn't long before Gran announced another game, this time we had to make something. "I've got enough rubber gloves for all you children including Emma. She will need some help, anyone up for that?"

"I'll help her Gran, she is my sister." announced Sam, taking the responsibility seriously.

"Great," said Gran. "I want you all to make a model of 'the Hand of Glory', is that ok with you all?"

"Is there a prize for the best one?" asked Sam.

"Yes, it's my parrot."

Olivia was the only one excited about the parrot but that didn't stop us from wanting to take part.

The task started out easy, all we had to do was fill the rubber glove with sand and pebbles, then squeeze it into shape. After that we had to colour it with dark green paint. Sam was the last to finish because he was helping Emma who was not being helpful at all. She preferred to flick the glove at Sam and annoy him.

I decided to help Sam out. Emma now decided she wanted to be lifted out of the hole she was sitting which Sam was relieved about. "At last I can now finish off both hands." stated Sam.

I started to walk away with Emma in my arms when Sam shouted. "Chris come and see this!"

I returned still holding Emma. "What is it Sam?" I asked.

"Look what Emma's been sat on all this time." In the hole was the black rock which Jack had first thought was the treasure. "I'm sure it's the skull of a dinosaur, a type of crocodile."

"Are you sure Sam, it just looks like rock to me."

"Yes, look at these holes, I think they are the eye sockets."

"Wow, we've got to tell Grandad. Come on Sam." Sam ran as fast as he could to the others while I followed still carrying Emma who at this point was clapping her hands and giggling, she bounced as I ran after Sam.

When I reached Sam he had already told everyone about the find and they were racing past me to see for themselves. Aunty Sarah took pity on me and took Emma from my arms. "Go on Chris join the others."

I didn't reply I just ran as fast as I could to catch the others up. We all started raking the sand back with our hands, sure enough the more we uncovered the more we were convinced that this was the remains of a dinosaur.

"Well we can't just keep this to ourselves we'll have to inform someone who's in the know." said Grandad. "Sam go and ask Mum for a phone and that museum leaflet we picked up the other day."

Sam shot off like a bullet. We carried on dragging the sand away from the black fossilised dinosaur. "What about the tide Grandad?" said Olivia as she pointed to the waves lapping onto the beach.

"I don't think it's going to be a problem, this top part of the beach never gets covered by the tide." replied Grandad.

Sam returned with a phone and the leaflet. Grandad dialled the museum's number and was soon explaining to someone what we had found. He was then put on hold, we all seemed to be on hold as well, as we waited in silence for the next person on the phone. Then Grandad responded, "Yes, well I'm not sure, you'll have to speak to Sam."

Sam looked surprised as Grandad handed him the phone. "They want to know what kind of dinosaur you think it is."

"Hello," said Sam holding onto the phone with both hands. "Well I think it might be a Deinosuchus," he paused then added. "No, it's definitely not an Ichthyosaurus, the head's too wide." Sam then started giggling excitedly, his voice getting louder as he continued to talk "Yes that's right we've got the head and we haven't finished uncovering the rest of it yet. Oh, yes I'll tell Grandad, thank you, bye."

"Well," said Grandad, "What is it you've got to tell me?"

"Well they can't believe we've found a complete skull let alone the rest of the body. The man said he was going to come here immediately."

"That's great, to think I found it and didn't know the importance of it." said Jack. "You amaze me Sam, you know so much about dinosaurs."

"Well I've been interested in palaeontology for years." said Sam as he walked back to the cottage in deep conversation with Jack. The tide was coming in fast now and Gran was waving to us to make our way back. The adults stayed put still looking at the hole and talking about the enormous size of this prehistoric animal. If Emma hadn't moved the stones and if Jack hadn't dug the hole and if Sam hadn't been so interested in palaeontology then it might never have been discovered. Wow!

CHAPTER 9

Professor York

Within twenty minutes we saw sight of a man walking on the beach heading straight for Grandad and the others. He stopped at the group and was shown the hole. He looked old and was dressed in a smart suit, not something you would wear on the beach. Gran came and stood next to us, "Well what are you all waiting for this is your find go and join the others." We ran down the steps and across the beach to see what was being said.

We didn't dare say anything at first, Grandad and the others were stood in silence watching the old man examine the find. It looked so out of place this old man dressed so smartly in the hole on his knees scraping back the sand from the black rock. "Where's the boy who said it was a Deinosuchus?" demanded the man.

"This is Sam," said Grandad as he placed his hand on Sam's shoulder. "He was the one who spoke to you on the phone." Grandad then looked down at Sam. "Sam this is Professor York."

Sam said nothing he looked overwhelmed at being singled out. "Well Sam," said the Professor, "I think we've got something amazing here. This could be one of the best finds ever in Britain and I'm very impressed that you knew what it was."

"So is it a Deinosuchus?" asked Sam.

"Well it looks like it, but we won't know for sure until we uncover a lot more." replied the Professor. He then stood up and turned to Grandad, "I will be starting the dig tomorrow, until then this part of the beach will be cordoned off."

Grandad helped him out of the hole and added, "We are stopping in one of the cottages over there," he pointed in the direction where Gran, Aunty Sarah and Emma were stood on the terraced gardens. "You and your team are welcome to use it as your base." Professor York thanked Grandad and headed back to the museum to organise the excavation.

We all headed back to the cottages. Gran was waiting, "Come on you lot the party isn't over yet." Jack and Joey's faces lit up, they thought the activities were at an end but I knew that when Gran starts something she likes to finish it and we hadn't had the judging of 'the Hand of Glory'.

Inside the cottage more food had replaced the empty and half empty plates. "Help yourselves," said Gran, "The judging of the hands will take place later, some are still wet and as for Emma's, well I don't think she'll mind missing out seeing as she didn't finish hers." We tucked into the feast without a thought of what had just taken place. The activities of the day had been both exciting and exhausting.

After we'd finished eating we decided to look out over the beach from the balcony. The tide was well in now but as Grandad had said our find was above the tide line. We were all talking about the dinosaur when we spotted a group of men with poles and netting approaching the hole. Professor York was in the midst of them showing them where he wanted the poles placed. The area that was being cordoned off was vast, far bigger than I'd thought would be fenced off. This was one fantastic find, probably the best kind of treasure ever.

We were all silent watching what was going on when Gran announced the judging of the hands was about to begin. We all moved down onto the terraced garden and stood by our efforts. Emma joined the judges, it was the only way Uncle John could keep her from wanting to go down onto the beach. Gran had devised a points system for all the adults and they were not allowed to give points to their own kids. Grandad said it was like the Eurovision song contest, whatever that was. Grandad knew a lot of things.

After all the totalling up from the judges and the pulling and poking of the exhibits from Emma, it was Olivia's hand that won the competition. Gran handed her the parrot with applauds from the rest of us.

"Well," said Grandad "I've had the best birthday ever, I don't know about you lot but none of what's happened today would have happened if it wasn't for Gran's treasure hunt. I think we need to give Gran a pirate's cheer." We all agreed and joined in shouting, "Hip hip hurray. Hip hip hurray. Hip hip hurray."

Gran blushed but enjoyed the attention. It was after this that we all decided to call it a day. It was late for the two little ones Sam and Emma, even Olivia was beginning to fade.

Jack asked if I wanted to go back with him for awhile, it sounded good. We spent most of the time looking out of the window watching the men put up the fencing and signs. We tried to guess what was written on the signs, it ended up a silly kind of game but one which had us rolling about in laughter.

It was gone 10pm when Jack's dad said he'd walk me back to Gran's. It was just a matter of crossing from one garden to another via a small wooden bridge. As I said thank you and goodnight to Jack and his dad I noticed that Professor York was still on the beach even though it was now very dark. There was someone with him but it wasn't a workman, this man was also in a suit. I guessed it was someone else from the museum.

CHAPTER 10

A house full

The following day was wet and dismal, not a day for going on the beach playing football. Not that that would have been allowed with the dig. And from what I could see from the balcony window there were a lot of people in wellies and waterproofs all busy moving buckets and buckets of sand from the hole. After breakfast Dad suggested I go with him to take Digger for a walk. I think he was shocked by my enthusiasm but the real motive was a chance to see how the dig was going.

Once on the beach I could at last see what the signs said. KEEP OUT, ARCHEOLOGICAL DIG IN PROGRESS, NO BALL GAMES and KEEP DOGS ON LEAD. The last one had me and Dad in stitches, we could just imagine Digger coming up out of the hole with a dinosaur bone in his mouth. Dad stopped to talk to one of the workers telling him that they were all invited to come up to the cottage for tea breaks and to use the toilet. They thanked us and two took us up on the offer straight away.

Back at the cottage Gran put the kettle on and Grandad busied himself making toast. Dad asked all kinds of questions about the dig all of it interesting but one thing stood out a mile, they were all excited about the prospect of it being a new species.

It wasn't long before Sam turned up, he'd been watching the comings and goings and persuaded his Dad that he might be of help. Sam was in his element discussing his thoughts about the find with people who knew something about the subject. Not like Gran who found it hard to pronounce some of the dinosaur names, although she loved that part of history. Aunty Zoë, being a history teacher, was far more in tune with him. As for the rest of us we looked to dinosaurs as the monsters in movies, although this new experience was different; it was exciting!

Although it was still raining we had the balcony doors open for all the comings and goings. The morning passed and lunch time was getting nearer. Grandad and Olivia headed off to the shops to buy more food, the visitors had wiped us out of bread and milk.

A knock on the glass doors startled me, everyone else had just walked in calling out 'hello' as they did so. I turned to see a group of people with cameras and notebooks, it was the press!

Dad and Gran stood up leaving their coffees on the table and stepped forward asking who they were and what did they want.

After the introductions Gran went to put the kettle on while Dad gave them the details as he knew it. When they started to ask how we knew it was such an important find that was when they were introduced to Sam.

Sam sat proud in his seat and answered all their questions. When they asked about who found the dinosaur Sam made a full and detailed reply. "I was the one who realised what it was, but it was my sister Emma who sat on it after Jack our friend had dug the hole. He dug the hole to look for the treasure that we were all looking for. It was my Grandad's birthday yesterday so we had a party for him, a pirates party. Gran organised a treasure hunt but when we got to the beach where the treasure was buried, Emma had moved the stones that covered the treasure. That's when we all had to dig holes, even Digger."

The reporters were getting a little lost from what Sam was saying, one asked the question again. "That's interesting Sam, but who was it that found it?"

Sam paused before answering. "Well, we all agreed to share the treasure once we found it. There was to be no mutiny, that we all agreed. So, everyone took part and therefore everyone should get the credit." The reporters looked blankly at each other but realised that that was the only answer they were going to get.

Grandad and Olivia turned up loaded down with shopping bags full of food. Followed closely by Uncle John who had called to tell Sam his lunch was ready.

"We'll leave it at that but is there a possibility we can call again should we need to?" enquired one of the reporters.

"I think that will be ok, but we are on holiday, you might not catch us in." replied Gran.

"Thank you for your time". said the reporter, followed by the others nodding and smiling as they backed out of the door.

A photographer quietly asked if he could take a photo of Sam by the dig. Uncle John was quickly put in the picture as to what had just taken place. "Well ok but his lunch is ready, will it be quick?"

"Dad, we all need to be in the picture other wise it'll be mutiny, won't it Grandad?" said Sam.

Grandad was still unpacking the bags. "That's right Sam, it's all or nothing."

"It's all or nothing!" stated Sam firmly.

"Can you call back later, in an hour or so and we'll see what we can do then." said Gran as though it was an every day occurrence.

The photographer nodded, then joined the others who were waiting outside on the balcony.

We all set too making sandwiches, more than we needed just in case we had more visitors.

Later Sam turned up again, this time with Aunty Sarah, Uncle John and Emma. Olivia had already let Jack and Joey know about the press and they were on their way. Before long the cottage was full again.

"What if they don't turn up?" said Olivia.

"Don't worry." said Grandad. "I've got my camera ready."

"Well what's stopping us from getting a picture now. We could do with something to remind ourselves of the treasure we found."

And so we all made our way down to the beach with our coats on as it was still raining. Dad chatted to the workers asking if it was possible to take some pictures. As Dad said earlier they could hardly say no when we'd fed them with tea and toast this morning. We got ourselves in position for Grandad to take the photo. For about five minutes Grandad snapped away until Dad stepped forward and said it was now Grandad's turn to get into the act. So then Dad took another few shots.

Looking at the work that had been done at the dig it was amazing. The whole of the skull had been uncovered and looked to be all in one piece. Work was now focused on the body. It had been explained to us that the sand was making it easy for them and that they hoped to remove the skull in just a day or two. We were lucky enough to have had the chance to see it before it disappeared into some laboratory to be examined fully. We were told that it would be a long time before it was put on show to the general public.

Finally the photographer turned up from the press. Another photo shoot and then we called it a day. We headed back to the cottage as the rain came down even heavier.

CHAPTER 11

Olivia's ghost story

The afternoon dragged, the rain didn't let up. We made the most of it playing board games. I missed having Jack and Joey around but they'd promised to call on us after tea. Emma thankfully had gone to sleep in the afternoon giving me, Olivia and Sam some time on our own.

Then Dad said he wanted me to go with him to get some fish and chips. I didn't mind, fish and chips was just what was needed on such a wet and cold day. Earlier he'd asked me to take Digger for a walk, that was a 'no deal'. I grumbled and made excuses; it worked, Dad went alone. Dad sent me next door to Aunty Sarah and Uncle John to see who wanted what. While there, Uncle James decided to help by coming along.

With plastic bags, lists and money we were ready to go. "Why are you taking plastic bags?" asked Olivia.

Grandad butted in, smiling as he did so, "We're all supposed to recycle as much as possible, that also means plastic bags. So we'll be supplying our own."

Olivia smiled and said, "Good for you Grandad, I've been trying to get the point over to Chris but with no luck."

I said nothing, it was a fight I knew I would lose. Still I'd won at least one battle this afternoon getting off with walking Digger.

Just as we were leaving, Dad handed me Digger's lead. "Well now that Uncle James is giving us a hand you won't mind taking Digger for a walk, will you."

He'd got me, I had no excuse this time.

Dad and Uncle James went off to the chip shop leaving me and Digger to follow on behind. Digger took advantage of my slow walk by stopping at every lamp post on route. We got to the corner that also lead onto the beach. "Come on Digger, lets see what's happening at the dig." As I thought, nothing. It was far too wet for the workers, but it didn't stop people, like myself, from going and having a look. The fence was a strong one, no one could get through it, but we could see deep down into the hole where the remains of the dinosaur were visible. With the very wet black fossilised rock against the yellow sand it looked magnificent. I was now pleased that I'd been the one picked to walk Digger.

We carried on a bit more then returned just in time for the fish and chips.

Jack and Joey came round soon after. Sam also joined us with some more of his board games. We all managed to make the most of the evening, only a few squabbles but we all remained friends. Then Gran asked if Jack and Joey wanted to sleep over. Our faces lit up. Jack and Joey hurried off to ask their Mum and Dad.

It was about an hour later when they returned with bedding and bags.

Grandad sorted out some DVD's for us to watch while Gran put together lots of finger food and goodies. The night was great, Mum and Dad had gone out with Aunty Sarah and Uncle John while Aunty Zoë and Uncle James babysat Emma. Sam also spent the night with us.

Gran and Grandad went to bed around 11pm, leaving us still wide awake and talking. On the windowsill was the 'Hand of Glory' exhibits from the day of the party. Jack said "Let's tell ghost stories."

I looked at Olivia as she looked at me and then Sam. "Well we've got a real story we can tell you about, it started one Christmas Eve with a game of hide and seek." I told Jack and Joey the whole story with a lot of help from Olivia and Sam. The story of when escaped prisoners gate crashed our party and how we rescued our parents from the evil intentions of the villains.

Sam was the first one to fall asleep, followed soon after by Olivia and Joey.

Me and Jack carried on talking but in a whisper. The memory of Christmas Eve brought back fears I'd not been able to talk to anyone about. Talking to Jack now felt good and helped me to open up about all the things I'd gone over in my mind, that might have happened if things had turned out differently. Then we heard a noise, it was coming from the back of the cottage where the street was. Someone was trying to open the door!

It turned out to be Mum and Dad! "Oh did we wake you?" said Mum.

"No we were just talking." I replied.

"Ok but don't leave it too late." said Dad. "Good night." At that they disappeared up the stairs.

Now one by one the others woke up wondering what was going on. So we decided to talk some more.

Olivia said she had a ghost story to tell so we settled down to listen. She pulled out a pink exercise book from her bag and opened it.

"Do you need a torch?" asked Jack handing her his.

"Thanks. It's about two boys called Jack and Ben who moved home with their parents to a very old house." She started to read.

'If you boys don't get up now, you are going to be left behind' warned mum as she rushed around the house trying to pack the last bits.

It was an early start on moving day and Jack and Ben were very excited, they would finally see the new house that mum and dad had been going on about. Apparently the new house was not new at all, it was in fact a very old house. Dad said it had character and more importantly a really big garage for his tools.

The new house wasn't much of a drive away, but it was still lots of fun for Jack and Ben to sit in the cab of the big van which dad drove while mum followed in the car. They both felt like giants looking down on the small cars in front.

When they arrived at the new house they were both shocked at how old the house looked. 'Blimey dad, it's a wreck' yelled Ben in astonishment.

'Yeah, it looks ancient' shouted Jack. But it didn't stop them from racing into the house as fast as they could to see which room was theirs. They nearly knocked over mum on their way ignoring her cries to be careful.

'Wow!' they cried in amazement.

'Look how big the staircase is!' Shouted Ben.

'It's huge!' gulped Jack.

They then ran up the stairs as fast as they could so that they could choose their room before mum and dad had a chance. Although it was dark and a bit gloomy upstairs, both boys felt comfortable with their new home. In fact it felt as if they had always lived there.

Without even talking to each other, they both walked towards the same room as if it had always been theirs. It was the only closed door on the landing, but they knew this was their room.

"That's spooky" whispered Sam.

"Shh." said Joey, eager to hear more.

Olivia continued. 'Mum and dad kept bringing in box after box into their room for them to unpack. As their dad brought in the last box which was piled high with books he tripped over the well worn rug that laid in the middle of the floor. The box spilled out all over the floor. Dad was ok but he shouted 'get rid of that stupid rug, it's dangerous'.

The boys picked up the books that were spread all over the floor. Then Jack got one end of the rug and Ben the other, they started to lift it in an effort to fold it over but it was incredibly heavy. 'It's like it's stuck to the floor', exclaimed Jack.

Finally with a lot of pulling and tugging the rug came free. To their surprise they found a trap door. 'How can that be, we are upstairs?' said Ben.

'Well let's open it and find out where it leads to.' replied Jack. Once opened they looked down a long stair case which seemed to go on forever. They quickly closed it again and looked at each other in amazement. 'What now?' Jack said in a whisper as though someone might hear him.

'What about looking to see what room is beneath this one.' said Ben.

'Yes let's go and see.' Jack lead the way, Ben quickly followed not wanting to be left alone in the room. Downstairs the room under their room was locked.

'Dad have you got the key to this room?' asked Ben.

'What room, what are you talking about.' replied dad. 'Come on you two there's work to be done.' Ben realised that dad couldn't see the door he was pointing to.

They raced back up to their room to find that the trapdoor had now disappeared."

Before Olivia could continue there was a flash of lightning followed by thunder. It was now the early hours of the morning, the rain got heavier followed by more thunder and lightning. Olivia had stopped telling her story too distracted by the rumbling of the storm and the lashing of the rain on the windows. We all sat up watching the storm without saying a word. The waves were pounding against the piers with such fury it was frightening.

Sam stood up to look down at the beach. "I wonder if the dig is alright it's bound to be full of water."

"Oh let me see Sam" said Olivia as she scrambled to her feet.

Both stood motionless with wide eyes and mouths open.

"What's wrong?" I asked.

Olivia spoke first "There's something moving along the beach."

"Yes it's enormous, I think it looks like a dinosaur, it could even be the ghost of the dinosaur from the dig." said Sam with excitement.

Looking out through the window we watched the dark shape move slowly towards the sea.

"Let's go out to have a closer look" said Joey. We looked at him as though he was mad. "Think about it, no-one's going to believe us unless we can prove it."

"Ok but how are we going to prove it, by capturing it!" exclaimed Jack.

"Why not," I said. "Let's ask Grandad to help us by taking a photo of it. That way we will capture it on camera and have the evidence and a witness."

"Won't he be angry?" asked Joey.

"No Grandad's ok, shall I wake him?" said Sam.

"Yes, you get Grandad while we get a closer look from the balcony."

"Don't go without me." Sam pleaded.

"We won't Sam. Oh and nobody turn the lights on because we need the darkness to see it better." So we all got our boots and coats on and opened the doors.

Sam was soon back with us followed by Gran and Grandad. We all watched the shape move from side to side as though caught in the movement of the wind. Grandad got his camera ready and took a number of shots without the flash. We were all quiet and motionless not really understanding what was happening.

Then I spotted a light in the water. It looked like a small boat. "Jack this doesn't look right."

Grandad said "Let's get nearer but be quiet we don't want whatever it is to see us."

I pointed out to Grandad the light on the waters edge. Grandad nodded and whispered something to Gran. She went back into the cottage and returned with our phones and some torches. "Now be careful" she said then returned to the balcony doorway. It was obvious she was staying at the window to keep watch.

We made our way down the steps without the use of the torches and in complete silence. Before going through the gate at the bottom of the garden Grandad turned our phones to silence.

We took each others numbers. We had no plan at this stage and we said very little. The storm was raging so much it covered up any noise that we might make. But our silence was more to do with the thought of what we might meet up with on the beach.

We slowly made our way along the side of the garden wall, Grandad leading the way. We stopped for Grandad to take more photos. The night was dark but the flashes from the lightning lit up the beach exposing the black shape of the large creature.

We saw the light again, flashing this time like a signal. As the lightning lit up the skies again we could see the small boat in the water bobbing up and down as the waves pushed it around like a toy.

Grandad motioned us to gather round him and to crouch down on the saturated sand. "We need to get closer but not all of us. We'll be spotted if there's too many of us."

"So who will go on with you Grandad?" I asked.

"Well I'm still not sure what it is we're facing here on the beach. Also there's the boat out there without onboard lights. And who is flashing that light from the boat and why?" Grandad paused for thought then continued. "Chris you come with me. Jack you stay here with the others. We will flash a torch once if we want you to take everyone back home, twice if we want you to come to us, but that will mean you on your own. That's when you Joey will need to stay put and look after Olivia and Sam."

No one objected, it wasn't the time or the place for squabbles. Grandad and me now moved forward on all fours, away from the cover of the wall. Grandad put his camera under his jacket. The shape was moving again, away from us and nearer to the boat. We moved on closer and closer. A flash of lightning sent us sprawling flat against the sand to avoid being seen. It was then that the beast was uncovered.

CHAPTER 12

The Beast

As Grandad and me lay there on the sand the truth about the beast was now clear, but it wasn't the end of the mystery. We were close enough to be sure that this was no beast. Under the moving shape we could see wheels!

Grandad now moved closer to me so we could whisper our conclusion. The beast was some kind of black covering over something with wheels.

"I don't like it Chris, why move something in the middle of the night and in the middle of a storm? Also if it's being moved to that boat, why isn't it lit up? And what's with the flashing lights from the boat?"

"Grandad they must be moving the dinosaur remains, they are the only thing of value around here."

"Well that's our treasure they're trying to take so let's get back to the others and see about stopping them." Grandad had a determined look on his face, he meant business.

We turned around and crawled back slowly looking behind us from time to time. Back with the others we shared our findings and our fears of what we felt was going on.

"So what now?" asked Jack.

"Chris, Sam and Olivia you head back to Gran and tell her to phone the police and coastguard. Me, Jack and Joey will stay here and watch."

The three of us kept close to the wall and moved slowly back to the steps. Once there, we virtually crawled up the steep steps to avoid being seen. We returned to Gran who was stood by the window of the cottage still in darkness.

I told Gran what me and Grandad had seen and that she was to phone the police and coastguard. She was right onto it without any hesitation.

When she'd put the phone down she turned to us and said "We can't let them get away with this, are you all up for a challenge?"

"What have you in mind Gran?" I asked.

"Well, I'll have to stay here for the police, Grandad and the others are watching from the beach. My fear is that once on the boat we'll lose them!"

"We could go to the pier and watch from there," I said.

"That's just what I had in mind," said Gran. "Then at least you'll be able to keep tabs on them from there. But be careful don't go right onto the pier, not in this storm"

"We'll be careful Gran don't worry. Come on you two we've got a dinosaur to stop." At that we left through the front door and up the cobbled street towards the pier. We stopped at the top of the hill to assess the best position to keep watch from and then proceeded down the walkway until we spotted the boat. Gran was right, with the storm nearly at an end the beast was now being lifted up onto the boat. We moved slowly along the ground on all fours, everything was wet and slippery. No one spoke, we knew our voices would carry, the only sound was from the squelching we made as we moved and the heavy panting as we struggled to breath under our wet hoods. At last we made it to the pier, having made a mad dash for the wall, one at a time. The sea was much calmer now and the rain had stopped.

We watched in the dark saying nothing.

It wasn't long before we saw the boat pull away from the beach. It chugged along not able to go any faster. It was very low in the water which was due to it's heavy load. As it turned away from us, heading for the open sea I told Olivia and Sam to watch it closely while I went to the other side of the pier wall to see which way it would turn once out past the breakwater.

It was a while before I spotted it. It still had no lights on but it was heading our way along the coast. "Come on let's get back and let Gran know which way it's going." I led the way up the path and along the street to the cottage.

"Chris," said Olivia as we reached the door. "What about watching where the boat goes from up there," pointing to the headland above us.

"Great idea," I replied. "You tell Gran what we've seen and me and Sam will go ahead."

"That's not fair. It was my idea." said Olivia sharply.

"Not now Olivia, you can follow on, we'll go up by the steps and along the fencing in the grave yard."

"I forgot about the grave yard," said Sam. "I'll tell Gran, you and Olivia can go."

"Thanks Sam, don't forget to tell Gran which way we've gone." said Olivia as we hurried off down the street.

CHAPTER 13

Pirates

Thankfully the street lights were still on, even up to the top of the steps.

"Be careful it's very slippery," I said as we climbed higher and higher until we reached the top.

We kept close together as we followed the fence along the cliff edge. The grave stones looked larger than ever. I reminded myself that there was nothing to be frightened of they were just graves, where dead people were buried. That did not help!

At the end we could see the boat tugging away along the coast. It had put it's lights on which made it easier for us to follow.

"Why has it put it's lights on now," asked Olivia.

"I think it's because it would look highly suspicious out there on the open sea. It just looks like any other boat now."

"But it's in the middle of the night, isn't that suspicious?"

"No Olivia, boats go out fishing through the night and come back in the morning with their catch."

"Oh, so now they look like any other fishing boat."

"Yes, but look we're going to lose them again, we'll have to go back."

We turned to follow the path back when we spotted some people in the distance.

"Quick, get down." I pulled Olivia down by my side as I said it.

"Who do you think it is Chris?"

"I don't know, we need to hide they're coming this way." I looked round then pointed to one of the grave stones. "You go behind that one there," I whispered.

Olivia's eyes were wide. "Where are you going Chris" she replied quietly.

"I'll go behind that one."

"Can't we share one."

"No, there's no time to get frightened of ghosts, we've got problems coming our way. Now go on and keep still."

So Olivia hid behind the grave stone I'd pointed out to her and I made for mine. I was now feeling scared but I couldn't let Olivia know it. I looked over to her and put my thumb up. She did the same to indicate she was ok.

There were five dark figures heading our way. As they came closer both Olivia and me slid down until we were lying flat on the graves themselves. Our fear had now transferred from our ghostly surroundings to the gang of men approaching.

They were talking quietly so I couldn't make out what they were saying.

Then a voice said. "Where can they be, Sam said they were coming up here."

It was Dad! We jumped up and shouted. The whole group which consisted of Dad, Uncle John, Uncle James, Jack and Joey all staggered back in fear.

We were just relieved it was family, we hadn't thought about how they would react to the two of us leaping up from the 'grave' as it were.

After the shock we explained where the boat was heading.

"Right," said Dad. "We'll carry on to the other side of the graveyard to see if we can see the boat from there. John you take Olivia home then join us there."

"No Dad, I want to come with you." replied Olivia hugging Dad as she did so. It always worked!

"Come on then. The four of us will go to the other side, while you James can take Jack and Joey through to the top road and see if you can spot them from there."

On our way I asked Dad, "Did the police turn up."

"Yes, that's why Grandad isn't here, they wanted a statement and for him to return to the site to explain everything."

"Where's Sam? I asked.

"The police are also questioning him about what he saw at the pier. That's when Gran sent for us."

"Are the police out looking for them as well?"

"Yes but best of all they've got the coastguard tracking them down. We've said we would inform them of anything unusual but the best of it is we might be able to see all the action from up here."

At the top end of the graveyard we watched the boat until it disappeared. "Right I'll let the others know that it's down to them to keep them in sight until we join them." said Dad as he pulled his phone out to call Uncle James.

We headed back across the graveyard to the top road where it followed the coast. We soon caught up with the others but Uncle James was missing.

"Jack where's James?" said Uncle John.

"He's gone down that track, he said we were to stay here and wait for you."

"Come on then let's go find him." said Dad.

It was darker than ever as we left the street lights behind. Dad told us we could use our torches but we had to keep them pointing to the ground, even a small light could be seen miles away. We walked in single file saying nothing, all our concentration was on where we put our feet. The narrow path was muddy and uneven.

We soon caught up to Uncle James. He pointed out to sea to where the boat was, then said, "The track carries on along the cliff edge so be careful, we'll carry on in single file."

Then Dad added, "You'll all have to switch off your torches now, they might spot us."

Slowly we continued, Olivia was behind me hanging onto the back of my jacket. Normally I'd have told her to let go, but this was no normal night, this was a night we were in pursuit of pirates.

CHAPTER 14

Saltwick Bay

We carried on for only a short while before encountering some kind of white building with a large ariel on top. It was all fenced off with no visible way of getting in. Not that we could see much without lights. Dad told us to keep low in case we could be spotted moving across the front of it. This we did without a single word spoken between us.

As we continued we could see some kind of bay with a beach. But that was not all. There seemed to be small buildings set out in rows. Dad decided to halt the group at this point. "The boat seems to be turning into that bay down there. I'm going to phone Gran and tell her to alert the police."

"Pete, they've turned their lights out again. You stay here while me and James get a bit closer to see what's happening." said Uncle John. Without a word I slipped away from the others and followed Uncle John and Uncle James.

The closer we got the clearer I could see the bay. It wasn't buildings I'd seen earlier it was caravans. As Uncle John and Uncle James stopped and crouched down in the thick grass to have a closer look I tapped Uncle James on the shoulder. He turned sharply with a look of horror on his face. "Chris!"

"Sorry, I just wanted to see for myself what the bay was like."

"Well you'd better text your Dad and tell him that you're with us and not fallen off the edge of the cliff." said Uncle James.

"And tell him there's a Land Rover and trailer driving onto the beach." added Uncle John, who had carried on watching the bay and caravan site.

I texted Dad then crouched close to Uncle John for a closer look. The Land Rover and trailer had driven past the caravans and was making it's way onto the beach. Close to the water's edge it stopped, then it's lights flashed. It was obviously a signal to the boat that they were there. Two men climbed out of the Land Rover and stood looking out to sea. The boat signalled back then turned towards the beach.

"Chris text your Dad and tell him and the others we need them up here quickly but quietly."

"Will do Uncle John." It wasn't long before Dad and the others were with us.

After a lot of whispering the plan was agreed. We were going to go down to the caravan site for a closer look. We went down in pairs apart from Olivia who insisted coming along with me and Dad. That made our trip the last one.

Once down amongst the caravans we could see the boat was as close as it could get to the beach. The two men were now wading out to the boat pulling the trailer with them. Dad pulled his phone out of his pocket to answer it. Thankfully it was on silent, we were now too close to make any sound. Dad did not reply, he closed his phone then texted his reply. We crouched in the dark waiting for him to tell us what the call was about.

" That was Gran," he whispered. "The police are on their way."

We turned to watch, as the men from the boat manoeuvred the dinosaur skull onto the trailer. Would the police get here in time? It must have been on everyone's mind because the next thing was Dad pulled us all well back from were we'd been watching the men and announced. "Look we need to stop these villains."

Olivia butted in quietly, "Dad they aren't villains, they're pirates."

"Yes you're right, anyway it's time to put the plan in motion." said Dad, so we all split up apart from Olivia who stayed with me. We fanned out around the edge of the caravan site then waited for a signal from Dad.

There it was, a flash from his torch. At that we all switched on our torches. Dad, Uncle John and Uncle James all started shouting. "Stop, this is the police, we have you surrounded." The men stopped in their tracks shielding their eyes from the torch lights. We thought we had them but the boat started to pull away leaving some of it's crew on the beach. One decided to make a run for it in mine and Olivia's direction, but the others held up their hands in surrender.

Then from out at sea we could see the flashing lights from the coastguard speeding to the boat that was trying to get away. That sight gave me and Olivia the incentive we needed. We looked at each other and knew what needed to be done.

Hand in hand we raced towards the man who was trying to get away. As we got level with the man I shouted out "Now". At that Olivia hurled herself in front of the man tripping him up. Then as he sprawled face first in the sand I dived on top of him pinning him on the ground. Olivia got to her feet and flashed her torch towards the others. Jack was the first one to get to us and joined in by sitting on the legs of the villain.

Within minutes the police arrived, sirens blaring and lights flashing. The man we were sat on was taken away grumbling something about kids. He looked familiar. We were all taken to the police station to give statements.

CHAPTER 15

The real pirate

At the police station we were given blankets and mugs of hot tea. We sat where we could, in the cramped office still buzzing from the events of the night. Me, Jack, Joey and Olivia were still wearing our pyjamas under our jackets, but that didn't seem to matter much.

As we chattered excitedly about what had taken place it dawned on me where I'd seen the man that me and Olivia stopped in his tracks. He was the one on the beach with the Professor. I stood up and asked to be interviewed next.

I gave my statement as I'd remembered and told them about the man talking to Professor York on the beach. The officer thanked me saying "That's the link we were looking for."

It was daylight when we left the police station, and only now that I was feeling embarrassed about being in my pyjamas. It was early but there were still a few people passing by giving us strange looks. The police gave us a lift back to the cottage where Mum and Gran were waiting for us. Jack and Joey went straight into there cottage where their Mum and Dad were glad to see them. Mum insisted we had a shower and off to bed. Gran asked if we wanted anything to eat. A bacon sandwich came to mind.

After a shower and the bacon butty we skipped sleep, we were still buzzing from the whole adventure. Gran kept on asking us questions, Mum just looked shocked at all she was hearing. Then a knock at the patio door stopped the conversation. It was the press.

We got the opportunity of telling our story one more time. Gran made more cups of tea for everyone and piles of toast.

We found out later from the police that Professor York was behind the piracy. He had hired the villains to steal the dinosaur's head and had arranged to sell it to someone in America.

After all the publicity we, including Jack and Joey, were given an extra weeks holiday for our part in the capturing of the pirates. The Mayor of Whitby held a banquet in our honour as a thank you for all we'd done. We were also given life time passes to the museum and the abbey.

It's a holiday we'll never forget.

Childrens Poems

My Pirate Poem
by Jake McMahon-Bates
from Broadway Primary School, Rossendale

Pirate Sam has a wooden leg,
Pirate Sam loves a boiled egg.

He has red eyes and is bad.
He has an enemy whose name is Chad.

They have a sword in their hand,
They like to fight all over the land.

Pirates

by Lucas Blanchard.
from Broadway Primary School, Rossendale.

Jolly Captain Slink,
Has never worn pink.

He has a golden earring,
which is swash-buckling.

If you act like a hog,
He'll throw you in the grog.

If you eat all the food,
He'll be in a right mood.

Captain Slink has a black patch,
That he wears in a footy match.

He carries round a sword,
In case he gets bored.

Pirate Bert
by Jordan Webb
from Broadway Primary School, Rossendale

I am a pirate I sail the seas,
I have black tatty pants from my hips to my
knees.

I have a striped shirt,
And my name is Bert.

The cannons blast,
While I climb the mast.

I like cheese,
And I'm allergic to bees.

A Pirates life

by Lewis Cooper
From Heap Bridge Village Primary School

A pirates life is the life for me,
Yo, ho, ho and a bottle of rum!
Dinosaurs will eat us all up for tea,
Yo, ho, ho, yum, yum yum!

We let the flag up into the sky,
Dinosaurs are here so were going to die!
Raise our glasses up really high,
Yo, ho, ho, ho, ho!

We travel across the open sea,
Yo, ho, ho it's time for tea!
Here they come we'd better flee,
Yo, ho, ho woohee!

Me pirate
by Summer EL Weshahai
From Heap Bridge Village Primary School

If I ever go to sea,
I think I'll be a pirate.
I'll wear an eye patch
And hook as sharp as a knife.

I will sail the seven seas
With my cutlass at my side.
Everyone will scream and shout
Whilst fleeing.

I will steal jewels and gold.
I will stash it in my treasure chest.
I will sail again to sea
And sail for ever and ever.

Pirates and Dinosaurs
by Charlie Thomas and Eleanor Fish
From Heap Bridge Village Primary School

Palm trees wave in the breeze,
Pirates sail on stormy seas.
Into land the death ship comes,
Out they come with full up tums.

Dinosaurs stomp on sandy ground,
Boy does that make a loud sound.
Dinosaurs break all the earth,
While their mother is giving birth.

The pirates fall in the dinosaurs trap,
The village of dinosaurs start to clap.
People hear vibrating in the floor,
Since the people came,
Pirates and dinosaurs are no more.

The war rages on
by Ellis Dixon
From Heap Bridge Village Primary School

The war rages on,
In the forgotten realms.
For the chosen one,
Who will rule all else.

Who fights in this war?
Why pirates and dinosaurs,
Disobeying the law,
In the land of the shore.
In this war two worlds collide,
Struggling for power,
Brought in by a furious tide...

Pirates, pirates
by Abbey Tattersall
From Heap Bridge Village Primary School

Pirates, pirates.
I am hunting you down.
Pirates, pirates,
I know your going to frown.

Pirates, pirates.
Your tough and sly.
Pirates, pirates.
I hope you are not shy.

Pirates fight
by Eliott Gotts

From St. Veronica's R.C. Primary School, Rossendale

Pirates fight day and night,
Plundering the seas to give you a fright.
Torturing you until you walk the plank,
Only euphoric when you have sank.

Dinosaurs are gigantic heavy beasts,
All their skin scaly and creased.
The thudding sound of their feet,
Gobbling every victim they meet.

But who would win or take the defeat,
If these two treacherous mammals were to meet.

Dinosaur poem
by James Hickson

From St. Veronica's R.C. Primary School, Rossendale

Daring to fight, trying their best,
In battles they are put to extreme tests.
Never giving up, dinos SNAP teeth,
On the go, eating meat like beef.
Shooting and crashing, bashing
And clashing.
Urging on and screaming ROAAR.
Ruthless and frightening, petrifying and
Scary, dinosaurs are!

Pirates

by Grace Enright
From St. Veronica's R.C. Primary School, Rossendale

Pirates, Pirates, grotty old things,
Daring dangerous a plan then rings!
"Let's capture gold, treasure and more,
Diamonds, Emeralds, let's start a war.

We'll sail the seven seas through night,
We'll curse them all, we'll start a fight
We maybe gruesome, greedy and more
But we're the best that's for sure.

We'll capture children, we'll steal gold,
We'll feed them green, spotty mould.
We'll then shout, 'hoy me hearties we are
The best'.
We'll open up the golden chest.

We'll make the children walk the plank,
We'll let them wash upon a river bank.
We'll drink beer and have a great big laugh".
Forgot to mention they don't have baths.

You now know what scruffy pirates do,
I've been put off them have you too?
Those smelly, terrifying, ugly rats
Come out in the dark, like bats.

Dinosaur Trouble

by Katie-Ann Barton

from St. James C.E. Primary School, Rossendale

Enormous feet with slimy bones,
Eating flesh and pinching phones.

Sharp white teeth with a spark for a smile,
Finding fossils from the Nile.

Some can fly and some just stand,
Can't even write with just one hand.

Always eats human meat,
They always come and feel the heat.

Eating boys throughout the day,
Never finish until May.

When there ill nose turns red,
Their body goes ridged and turns to lead.

A dinosaur's brain might be small,
But don't think fine, not at all.

One-eyed Pete
by Charlotte Burke

From St. Veronica's R.C. Primary School, Rossendale

Their ship sails the seven seas,
The men you wouldn't dare to tease.
Skull and crossbones flying high,
In the misty moonlit sky.
"Ahoy there!" growled One-eyed Pete,
His platted beard down to his feet.
"How dare you come upon my ship!"
He pulled his sword from by his hip.
His bloodlust crew climbed down the rigging,
To attack the intruder, without thinking.
It's best to stay away from these lads,
If not, your life they could have....

Pirates sing

by Hazera Begum

From St. James C.E. Primary School, Rossendale

Pirates sing their jolly song,
But dinosaurs really reek and pong.
Pirates love stealing things,
But dinosaurs are mighty Kings.
Pirates like finding buried treasure,
Dinosaurs are a mighty measure.
Pirates look really weird,
Dinosaurs are all cleared.

There once was a Pirate named Peg
by Faizah Hanif

From St. James C.E. Primary School, Rossendale

There once was a pirate named Peg,
He had a rotten wooden leg.
When he was in a race,
He fell on his face.
That stupid old pirate named Peg.

There once was a pirate named Jones

by Tanjimul Hoque and Sahariah Miah
From St. James C.E. Primary School, Rossendale

There once was a pirate called Jones,
Whose ship flew the skull and cross bones.
He wore an eye patch,
That made him scratch.
The spotty old pirate called Jones.

Things gone
by Paul Meynell
From Haslingden High School, Rossendale

Pirates there were many, years and years ago.
They didn't have any engines and so they had to
row.

Many angry pirates, travelling stormy seas,
Dinosaurs eating birds, straight out of the trees.

Pirates on an island, digging deep for gold.
It is more expensive, especially as it's old.

Pirates in the North Sea, putting up their sail.
Weren't looking where they were going, crashed
into a whale.

A pirate standing proud, travelling in his galleon.
Like a nautical cowboy, riding a black stallion.

Pirates are evil and tough, or so it's often said.
But we know that their mums still tuck them up
in bed!

The Pirates Express

by Sameera Akhtar and Ciera McDermott
From Haslingden High School, Rossendale

Pirates, pirates
All aboard.
The Pirates Express is ready to go.

Music, violence, singing and rum,
All we can do is shout and hum,
Pirates, pirates
All aboard.
The Pirates Express is near to shore.

"Shiver me timbers" is what we say,
We shout, "Aaargh," to scare you away.
All aboard.
The Pirates Express is at the shore.

Scruffy ratbags,
That's what we are,
With wooden legs and eye patches.
We travel so far.

Pirates, Pirates.
All aboard.
The Pirates Express is heading home.

They look for treasure
by Umairah Malik
From St. James C.E. Primary School, Rossendale

They look for treasure all around,
But with no idea where it can be found.
Sailing ships,
On their long winding trips.
Although they're not very clever,
Pirates will always be about forever!

My dinosaur called Felly

by Lianne Rose Jamieson

From Whalsay Primary School, The Shetlands

My dinosaur, it's very small and not that fat.

It loves dogs and not cats.

He's very cool and swims in a pool.

He's always chatting and likes stomping and
clapping.

His name is Felly and he wiggles his belly.

He's very smart and loves to fart.

He's very nosy and his best friend is Rosie.

His sister is May and she likes playing with clay.

He is very pale and has a long tail.

Why we don't see T-Rex today

Story created by the reception class at
Whalsay Primary School, The Shetlands

There was once a T-Rex, a shark and a crocodile who lived together. They all had sharp teeth and were always hungry.

One day, after eating all their meat they still wanted more. So they went to a café and ordered some fish and chips. After this the shark and the crocodile ate cakes but the T-Rex decided he wanted sweets. They were all so full that they went outside and laid on the grass to rest their very full bellies.

While they were sleeping a meteor came crashing out of the sky, the shark and the crocodile managed to dive into the river near by but the T-Rex didn't make it. So that's why you don't see T-Rex today.

If you enjoyed this story the previous adventure
in this series is still available:

A game of hide and seek

"a game of hide and seek" starts with a family get
together on Christmas Eve. As the adults continue
to party the children, along with Gran, decide
to play the game hide and seek. While hiding in
the cellar a knock at the door turns their game
into a survival plan. The callers turn out to be
escaped prisoners and decide to do some hiding
themselves and chose Gran's house to do it in.

To contact Irene please email her at:
farrimonds@hotmail.co.uk or visit the website:
www.threewhitefoxes.com